GAME OVER

by Benjamin Bird

illustrated by Patrycja Fabicka

raintree

a Capstone company — publishers for children

Raintree is an imprint of Capstone Global Library
Limited, a company incorporated in England and
Wales having its registered office at 264 Banbury
Road, Oxford, OX2 7DY – Registered company
number: 6695582

www.raintree.co.uk
myorders@raintree.co.uk

ISBN 978 1 3982 0250 4

Designed by Sarah Bennett
Originated by Capstone Global Library Ltd
Printed and bound in the United Kingdom

Acknowledgements
Shutterstock: ALEXEY GRIGOREV, design element, vavectors, design
element, Zaie, design element

British Library Cataloguing in Publication Data
A full catalogue record for this book is available from the
British Library.

CONTENTS

CHAPTER ONE
▶ PRESS START ◀

A boy raced through a long, brick maze.

"HUFF! HUFF!"

He struggled to breathe, but the boy could not rest. Something was chasing him.

The boy heard heavy footsteps close by.

THOMP! THOMP! THOMP!

He sped round a sharp corner and came face to face with a giant beast!

The monster showed its sharp fangs.

"ROOAAAAR!"

Arthur screamed in his
bedroom. He threw his video
game controller onto the
carpet. The game's final boss
had beaten him again.

"I'll never defeat the
Maze Monster!" Arthur
whined.

Arthur pressed the game's POWER button, but the machine wouldn't turn off. He pushed the button again – and then again.

An alert popped up on the TV screen. It read: YOU HAVE ONE LIFE REMAINING.

Arthur scratched his head, confused.

How did I get an extra life? he wondered.

Then another message flickered on the screen: PRESS START TO CONTINUE . . . IF YOU DARE!

CHAPTER TWO
LEVEL UP

"Awesome! A bonus life!" Arthur smiled with delight.

A countdown began on the TV: "5 . . . 4 . . . 3 . . . 2 . . ."

With one second left, Arthur jammed his thumb on the START button.

CLICK! Suddenly, everything went dark.

"Mum!" Arthur yelled. "The power has gone off again!"

But nobody answered.

Arthur grunted. "I really hope my game saved."

Arthur stood and stumbled
through the dark. He searched for
a light switch. He didn't find one.

Instead, Arthur tripped and fell.
His bedroom floor felt like bricks.

"Ouch!" he cried.

The floor was bricks! When
Arthur looked up, lots of arrows
glowed in front of him.

The arrows pointed towards
a steel door marked with
two words: FINAL BOSS!

"What is happening?"
Arthur asked, puzzled.

FWOOSH! The door flung open.
Arthur got up, brushed himself off
and walked through the entrance.
An endless maze awaited him.

It can't be, thought Arthur, looking around. *I'm in the video game!*

WHAM! The steel door slammed shut behind him. Everything went silent. Then Arthur heard a sound from within the maze.

THOMP! THOMP! THOMP!

"The Maze Monster!" he cried.

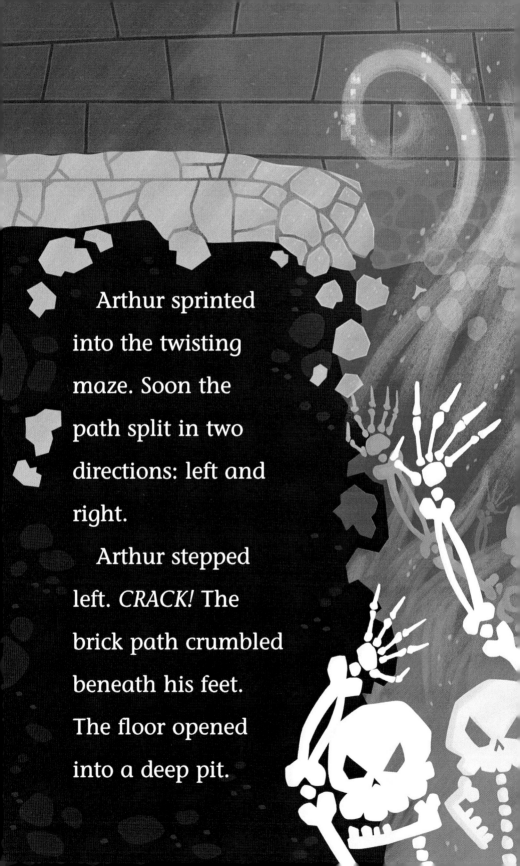

Arthur sprinted into the twisting maze. Soon the path split in two directions: left and right.

Arthur stepped left. *CRACK!* The brick path crumbled beneath his feet. The floor opened into a deep pit.

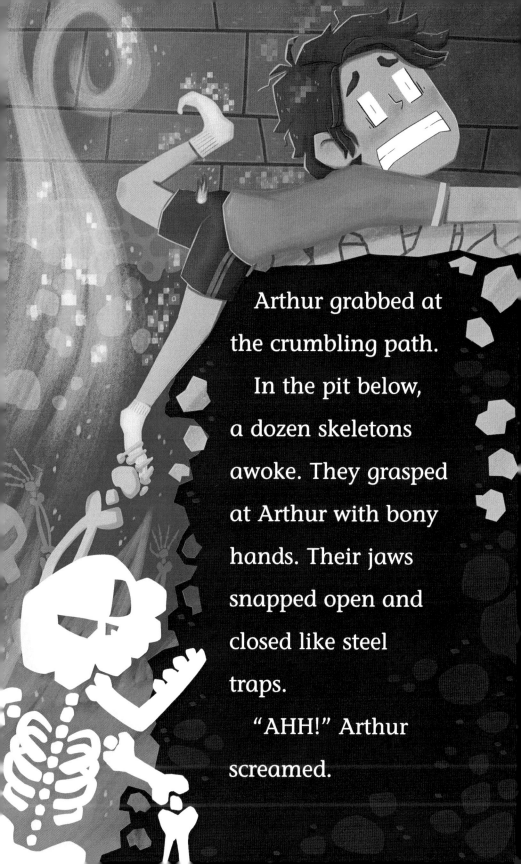

Arthur grabbed at the crumbling path. In the pit below, a dozen skeletons awoke. They grasped at Arthur with bony hands. Their jaws snapped open and closed like steel traps.

"AHH!" Arthur screamed.

CHAPTER THREE
FINAL BOSS

Arthur pulled himself up and crawled safely away from the pit.

"Beginner's mistake," he said, shaking his head.

Arthur looked around again.

"Think," he told himself. "You've played this level before."

This time, Arthur headed right instead of left. The floor did not crumble.

As he ran, Arthur remembered the correct path. But with each twist and turn, the footsteps grew louder.

THOMP! THOMP! THOMP!

Then, up ahead, the path turned sharply. Arthur stopped.

The footsteps stopped too.

Arthur pressed his back against the brick wall. He inched closer to the turn.

He could hear the Maze Monster breathing around the corner.

Suddenly, one of the bricks on the wall moved. Arthur pushed on it, and a secret drawer opened.

He reached inside and pulled out a flaming sword!

"Power up!" Arthur exclaimed.

With the sword, Arthur turned
the corner. He came face to face
with the giant beast again.

SLASH! Arthur swung his sword
at the monster.

FWOOSH! The beast lashed out
with its claws.

The fighting went on. And on. And on.

Both Arthur and the Maze Monster were growing weak. One final blow would destroy either one of them.

SLASH! FWOOSH!

Then, suddenly, everything went dark again.

Back in his bedroom, a door slowly opened.

CREAK!

Arthur's mother yelled up, "Is everything okay, Arthur?"

No one answered. But on the TV screen, a final message flashed: GAME OVER.

AUTHOR

Benjamin Bird is a children's book editor and freelance writer from Minnesota, USA. He has written books about some of today's most popular characters, including Batman, Superman, Wonder Woman, Scooby-Doo, Tom & Jerry and many more.

ILLUSTRATOR

Patrycja Fabicka is an illustrator with a love for magic, nature, soft colours and storytelling. Creating cute and colourful illustrations is something that warms her heart – even during cold winter nights. She hopes that her artwork will inspire children, as she was once inspired by *The Snow Queen, Cinderella* and other fairy tales.

alert a signal of danger

defeat to win a victory over something

destroy to put an end to something

endless being or seeming to be without end

fang a long, sharp tooth

final boss the last opponent in a video game

1. Do you think Arthur lost to the Maze Monster? Why or why not?

2. Look back through the book. What illustration do you think is the scariest? Explain.

3. What is your favourite video game to play? Explain your choice.

WRITING PROMPTS

1. Writing scary stories can be a lot of fun! Try writing your own scary story to share.

2. Draw a monster. Then give the monster a name and write a few sentences about it.

3. Write a paragraph about the scariest dream you've ever had.

SCARED SILLY JOKES!

What kind of vehicle does the Maze Monster drive?
a monster truck

What is the best way to speak to the Maze Monster?
from far, far away

What does the monster use to keep his maze cool on hot days?
a scare conditioner

Why are cats so good at video games?
They have nine lives.

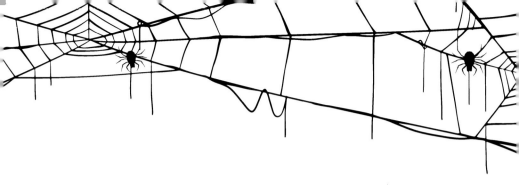

What is the Maze Monster's favourite type of bean?

human beans

What do you call a friend who doesn't let you play a video game?

a control freak

BOO BOOKs

Discover more just-right frights!

CLOWNS FROM OUTER SPACE

GAME OVER

SLIME TIME!

SWAMP CREATURE TEACHER

ATTACK OF THE CUTE

CAMPFIRE VAMPIRE

THE HAUNTED BACKPACK

NIGHT OF THE DIGGING DOG

SCARE BALL

WITCH'S STEW

Only from Raintree